SAY GOOD NIGHT!

For A. M. B., who knows
good dreams come on good nights

PUFFIN BOOKS
Published by the Penguin Group
Penguin Books USA Inc., 375 Hudson Street, New York, New York 10014, U.S.A.
Penguin Books Ltd, 27 Wrights Lane, London W8 5TZ, England
Penguin Books Australia Ltd, Ringwood, Victoria, Australia
Penguin Books Canada Ltd, 10 Alcorn Avenue, Toronto, Ontario, Canada M4V 3B2
Penguin Books (N.Z.) Ltd, 182-190 Wairau Road, Auckland 10, New Zealand

Penguin Books Ltd, Registered Offices: Harmondsworth, Middlesex, England

First published in the United States of America by Viking Penguin Inc., 1987
Published simultaneously in Puffin Books
Published in a Puffin Easy-to-Read edition, 1995

1 3 5 7 9 10 8 6 4 2

Text copyright © Harriet Ziefert, 1987
Illustrations copyright © Catherine Siracusa, 1987
All rights reserved

THE LIBRARY OF CONGRESS HAS CATALOGED THE VIKING PENGUIN EDITION UNDER
THE CATALOG CARD NUMBER 86-46220.

Puffin Books ISBN 0-14-036839-6

Puffin® and Easy-to-Read® are registered trademarks of Penguin Books USA Inc.
Printed in the United States of America

Reading Level 1.4

SAY GOOD NIGHT!

Harriet Ziefert
Illustrated by Catherine Siracusa

PUFFIN BOOKS

Now say good night,
they say.
Now say good night.

But I don't want
to say good night.

Why *good?* I ask.
What's good
about the night?

Tell me.

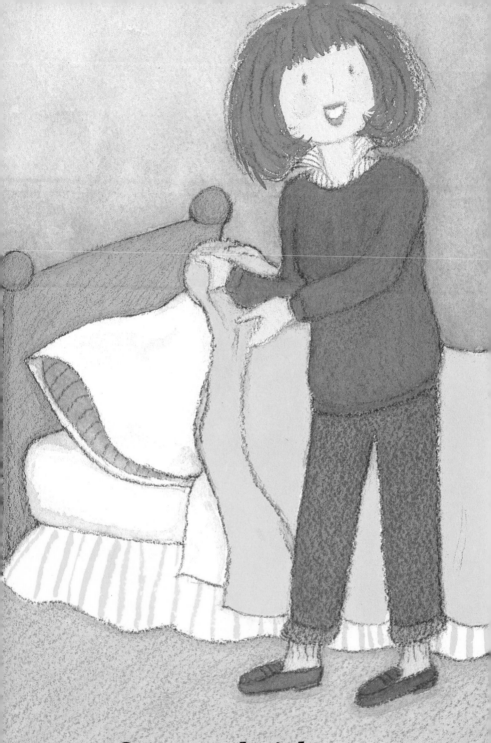

On a good night
you can see the moon.

And moons are nice.

On a good night
you can hear quiet.

And quiet is nice.

Warm breezes come
on good nights.

And breezes are nice.

Good dreams come
on good nights.
And dreams are nice.

So say
good night.
Good night
good night
good …

night!

All right, good night!
Turn off my light.

Sleep tight
Sleep tight
Till morning light.

Now say good morning,
they say.
Now say good morning.

Why *good?* I ask.
What's good
about the morning?

On a good morning
you can see the sun.

You can smell
bacon and eggs

and hear music
from the radio.

So say
good morning.

Good morning good
morning good…

morning!

All right, good morning!

I'm up!